Hello, Family Members,

Learning to read is one of the most important accomplishments of early childhood. **Hello Reader!** books are designed to help children become skilled readers who like to read. Beginning readers learn to read by remembering frequently used words like "the," "is," and "and"; by using phonics skills to decode new words; and by interpreting picture and text clues. These books provide both the stories children enjoy and the structure they need to read fluently and independently. Here are suggestions for helping your child *before*, *during*, and *after* reading:

Before

- Look at the cover and pictures and have your child predict what the story is about.
- Read the story to your child.
- Encourage your child to chime in with familiar words and phrases.
- Echo read with your child by reading a line first and having your child read it after you do.

During

- Have your child think about a word he or she does not recognize right away. Provide hints such as "Let's see if we know the sounds" and "Have we read other words like this one?"
- Encourage your child to use phonics skills to sound out new words.
- Provide the word for your child when more assistance is needed so that he or she does not struggle and the experience of reading with you is a positive one.
- Encourage your child to have fun by reading with a lot of expression . . . like an actor!

After

- Have your child keep lists of interesting and favorite words.
- Encourage your child to read the books over and over again. Have him or her read to brothers, sisters, grandparents, and even teddy bears. Repeated readings develop confidence in young readers.
- Talk about the stories. Ask and answer questions. Share ideas about the funniest and most interesting characters and events in the stories.

I do hope that you and your child enjoy this book.

—Francie Alexander
Reading Specialist,
Scholastic's Instructional Publishing Group

To All the Kids at
Wedgewood School
—K.M.

To Ainsley
—M.S.

Text copyright © 1998 by Kate McMullan.
Illustrations copyright © 1998 by Mavis Smith.
All rights reserved. Published by Scholastic Inc.
SCHOLASTIC, HELLO READER! and CARTWHEEL BOOKS and associated logos
are trademarks and/or registered trademarks of Scholastic Inc.

Library of Congress Cataloging-in-Publication Data
McMullan, Kate.
    Fluffy saves Christmas/by Kate McMullan; illustrated by Mavis Smith.
      p.   cm. — (Hello reader! Level 3)
    "Cartwheel books."
    Summary: Fluffy the class guinea pig shares the Christmas party at school; goes home for the holidays with Jasmine; and meets Santa twice, once at the mall and once in a dream.
    ISBN 0-590-52308-2
    [1. Guinea pigs — Fiction. 2. Christmas — Fiction. 3. Santa Claus — Fiction. 4. Dreams — Fiction. 5. Schools — Fiction.]   I. Smith, Mavis, ill.   II. Title.   III. Series.
  PZ7.M47879Flf   1998
  [E] — dc21   98-24127
                                                                              CIP
                                                                              AC
10 9 8 7 6 5 4 3   9/9 0/0 01 02 03 04

Printed in the U.S.A.   24
First printing, November 1998

FLUFFY
SAVES CHRISTMAS

by Kate McMullan
Illustrated by Mavis Smith

Hello Reader! — Level 3

SCHOLASTIC INC.
New York   Toronto   London   Auckland   Sydney

Fluffy Cookies

Ms. Day's class was making cookies
for their Christmas party.

Fluffy was asleep in his cage.
In his dream,
some big, bad guinea pigs
were stealing Christmas presents.
Stop, Cruncher!
Fluffy told the biggest pig.
**Or I will take you
and your brothers in!**

Jasmine was rolling out cookie dough.

Wade sat down beside her.

"Uh-oh," said Wade. He stood up.

"I just sat on the sheep cookie-cutter!"

"Give it to me," said Jasmine.

"I will fix it for you."

Jasmine pulled on the
sheep cookie-cutter.
"There," she said.
"Does it look like a sheep?"
"No," said Wade.
"It looks like Fluffy."

Wade pressed the Fluffy cookie-cutter
into the cookie dough.
He put his Fluffy cookie
on a cookie sheet.
"I want to make a Fluffy cookie,"
said Jasmine.
"Me, too," said Emma.
"Me, three," said Maxwell.

Meanwhile, Fluffy was dreaming
that he caught the big, bad guinea pigs.
He tied them up and took them in.
It's Cruncher and his bad brothers!
said the Guinea Pig Police Chief.
Nice work, Fluffy!

Everyone in Ms. Day's class
made a Fluffy cookie.
Ms. Day baked the cookies and
the kids iced them.
They stuck on chocolate bits for eyes.
They shook on sprinkles.

"Let's show Fluffy," said Jasmine.
The kids lined up their cookies.
Jasmine took Fluffy out of his cage.
"Hey, Fluffy!" she said.
"Check out our Christmas cookies!"

Fluffy did not want to wake up
from his good dream.
Slowly he opened his eyes. Yikes!

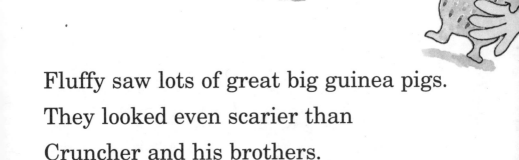

Fluffy saw lots of great big guinea pigs.
They looked even scarier than
Cruncher and his brothers.

Back off, pigs! Fluffy growled.
The pigs just stared at Fluffy.
All right, Fluffy said. **You asked for it!**
With a terrible growl, Fluffy charged.

The kids quickly picked up
their Christmas cookies.
Jasmine put Fluffy back in his cage.
"I don't think Fluffy likes cookies," she said.

"Time for our Christmas party!" called Ms. Day.
She poured punch into cups.
Then the kids ate their cookies.

They nibbled the feet.

They nibbled the ears.

They bit off the heads.

Fluffy watched the kids eat up

all the great big guinea pigs.

I must still be sleeping! thought Fluffy.

And having a crazy Christmas dream!

Fluffy Meets Santa

Fluffy went home with Jasmine
for Christmas vacation.
Maxwell and Violet came by.
"We are going to see Santa,"
Violet told Jasmine.
"Let's take Fluffy to see Santa, too."
"Okay," said Jasmine.
And off they went to the mall.
Who is Santa? Fluffy wondered
on the way there.
What is Santa?

Jasmine, Maxwell, and Violet
waited to see Santa.
Fluffy peeked out of his box.
He saw that Santa was big.
Santa had a furry face.
Santa made funny noises:
Ho ho ho!

"I'm Violet," Violet told Santa
when it was her turn.
"And this is Fluffy."
"Ho ho ho!" said Santa.
"Have you been a good little guinea pig, Fluffy?"
Are you kidding? thought Fluffy.
I'm the best guinea pig in the world!

"Santa," said Violet,

"Fluffy is going to tell you

what he wants for Christmas."

I am? thought Fluffy.

Violet held Fluffy up to Santa's ear.

Uh..., thought Fluffy.

What have you got?

"Ho ho ho!" Santa boomed.

"Fluffy wants a great big carrot

for Christmas!"

Good guess, thought Fluffy.

He waited for Santa to give him

the great big carrot.

Violet sat on Santa's knee.

She held Fluffy on her lap.

"Ho ho ho!" said Santa.

"What do you want for Christmas, Violet?"

"I want a puppy and a pony," said Violet.

Hey, Santa! thought Fluffy.

What about my carrot?

Violet kept talking to Santa.
So Fluffy decided to find
the great big carrot himself.
He stepped off Violet's lap.
He walked up Santa's belly.
He crawled under Santa's face fur
and inside Santa's shirt.

"I want a baby monkey, too,"
Violet told Santa.

Suddenly Santa cried, "Ho ho HO! Something
is tickling me!" Violet hopped off Santa's lap.

Santa jumped up. "Ho ho hee hee!"
Santa laughed.

Santa kept laughing. "Ho ho hoo!"

"Violet?" said Jasmine.

"Where is Fluffy?"

"I don't have him," said Violet.

"Uh-oh," said Jasmine.

"Ho ho whoa!" Santa cried.

He pulled off his hat.

"There's Fluffy," cried Violet,

"on Santa's head!"

Santa took Fluffy off his head.

He looked Fluffy in the eye.

Where is my carrot? thought Fluffy.

My great big carrot?

"Ho ho ho!" said Santa.

Fluffy Saves Christmas

Carolers came to Jasmine's house
on Christmas Eve.
Fluffy listened to them sing
The Night Before Christmas.

The song told how Santa flew in a sleigh
pulled by reindeer.
Santa landed on rooftops.
He slid down chimneys.
He filled stockings.
He left presents for everyone
under the Christmas tree.
When he was finished,
he called to his reindeer:
"On Dasher! On Dancer!
On Prancer and Vixen!
On Comet! On Cupid!
On Donner and Blitzen!
To the top of the roof!
To the top of the wall!
Now dash away! Dash away!
Dash away all!"

When the carolers left,
Jasmine got into her pajamas.
"Good night, Fluffy," she said.
"Tomorrow is Christmas!"

Fluffy curled up in his cage.
He was almost asleep when
he heard someone call, "Fluffy!"
It was Santa!
"I can't deliver my presents tonight,"
Santa told Fluffy.

Why not? asked Fluffy.

"I have the flu," said Santa.

"And so do all my reindeer."

Don't worry, Santa, said Fluffy.

I will deliver the presents for you.

Fluffy ran over to the
Guinea Pig Police Station.
Cruncher, said Fluffy.
**if you and your brothers will
be good from now on,
you can pull Santa's sleigh tonight.**

We promise! said all the brothers.

Fluffy hitched the big guinea pigs
to Santa's sleigh.
They pulled Fluffy through the sky.
They landed on rooftops.
Fluffy slid down chimneys.
He filled stockings.
He left presents for everyone.

When he finished,
Fluffy called to his team:
On Cruncher! On Muncher!
On Snacker and Fuzzy!
On Chubby! On Tubby!
On Squeaky and Wuzzy!
To the top of the roof!
To the top of the wall!
Now dash away! Dash away!
Dash away all!

"Wake up, Fluffy!" Jasmine said.

"It's Christmas!"

Fluffy opened his eyes.

Jasmine said, "Come see

what Santa brought you!"

Jasmine carried Fluffy over to the
Christmas tree.
And there, with a red bow tied around it,
was the biggest carrot
Fluffy had ever seen.

"Merry Christmas, Fluffy!" said Jasmine.

Ho ho ho! thought Fluffy.

Merry Christmas!

2/7   12/03   1-13-04